RICKY RICOTTA'S MIGHTY ROBOT

VS. THE VIDEO VULTURES FROM VENUS

STORY BY
DAV PILKEY

ART BY
DAN SANTAT

SCHOLASTIC INC.

FOR CAMERON
JAMES CHRISTOPHER
– D.P.

FOR JAIME T.
(THANKS FOR ALL THE HELP)
– D.S.

Text copyright © 2001, 2014 by Dav Pilkey
www.pilkey.com

Illustrations copyright © 2014 by Dan Santat
www.dantat.com

All rights reserved. Published by Scholastic Inc., *Publishers since 1920.*
SCHOLASTIC and associated logos are trademarks and/or registered trademarks of Scholastic Inc.

The publisher does not have any control over and does not assume any responsibility
for author or third-party websites or their content.

No part of this publication may be reproduced, stored in a retrieval system, or transmitted
in any form or by any means, electronic, mechanical, photocopying, recording, or otherwise,
without written permission of the publisher. For information regarding permission, write to
Scholastic Inc., Attention: Permissions Department, 557 Broadway, New York, NY 10012.

This book is a work of fiction. Names, characters, places, and incidents are either the product
of the author's imagination or are used fictitiously, and any resemblance to actual persons,
living or dead, business establishments, events, or locales is entirely coincidental.

Library of Congress Cataloging-in-Publication Data Available

Originally published as *Ricky Ricotta's Mighty Robot vs. the Voodoo Vultures from Venus*

ISBN 978-0-545-63011-5

24 23 22 21 20 19   20 21 22 23

Printed in China   62

Book design by Phil Falco

CHAPTERS

CHAPTER ONE
LATE FOR SUPPER

It was suppertime at the Ricotta home. Ricky's father was sitting at the table. Ricky's mother was sitting at the table. But Ricky was not sitting at the table.

And neither was his Mighty Robot.

"It is six o'clock," said Ricky's father. "Ricky and his Mighty Robot are late for supper again."

Just then, Ricky and his Mighty Robot flew in.

"Sorry we are late," said Ricky. "We were in Hawaii collecting seashells."

"You have been late for supper three times this week," said Ricky's mother. "No more TV until you boys learn some responsibility."

"No TV?" cried Ricky. "But *Rocket Rodent* is on tonight. Everybody on Earth will be watching it!"

"Everybody but you two,"
said Ricky's father.

CHAPTER TWO

RESPONSIBILITY

That night, Ricky and his Mighty Robot went to bed early. They camped in the backyard under the stars.

"I sure wish we could watch TV tonight," said Ricky.

Ricky's Robot unscrewed his hand,
and out popped a big-screen television.
"No, Mighty Robot," said Ricky.
"We're not allowed. We've got to learn
some responsibility first."

Ricky's Mighty Robot did not know what *responsibility* was.

"*Responsibility*," said Ricky, "is doing the right thing at the right time."

Ricky and his Mighty Robot were pretty good at doing the right thing . . .

. . . but they had trouble
with the *right time* part.

15

CHAPTER THREE
VICTOR VON VULTURE

At that very moment, almost twenty-five million miles away, there lived an evil vulture on the planet Venus.

TEMPERATURE: 864 DEGREES

ONLY 2,915 HOURS TILL SUNSET!

TODAY'S FORECAST:
MOSTLY GASSY
(WITH A CHANCE OF
SULFURIC ACID).

His name was Victor Von Vulture,
and he hated living on Venus.

It was so hot on Venus that everyone's food was always ruined. Their grilled cheese sandwiches were always *way too gooey* . . .

. . . they had to drink their candy
bars with straws . . .

. . . and everybody's ice cream melted before they could even get one lick!

So Victor Von Vulture decided
to move to Earth where the
eatin' was good.

First, he invented the Video-Schmideo 2000. Then he climbed aboard and went looking for an army.

HAW HAW

HAW HAW

NOW LISTEN UP, BIRD BRAINS!

WHEN I PRESS THIS BUTTON, A VIDEO BEAM WILL SHOOT THROUGH SPACE...

CHAPTER FOUR
VIDEO RAYS FROM OUTER SPACE

Ricky and his Mighty Robot fell asleep under the stars, while everyone else in town was watching television.

Suddenly, a video ray from outer space beamed down through the night sky. The strange signal was picked up by all the TVs in town.

The screens began to glow eerily as a strange voice came from the wicked signal.

"Obey the Video Vultures!" said the voice. "Obey the Video Vultures!"

Soon, every mouse in the city
was hypnotized.

CHAPTER FIVE
BREAKFAST WITH THE ROBOT

The next morning, Ricky woke up and went inside to fix breakfast. But all the food in the house was gone.

"Hey!" said Ricky. "Where's all the food? I can't go to school without breakfast!"

Ricky's Robot knew just what
to do. He flew straight to Florida.
A few seconds later, he returned
with an orange tree.

"Thanks, Mighty Robot," said Ricky. "I love fresh-squeezed orange juice! Now, may I have a doughnut?"

Ricky's Mighty Robot flew off again. Soon he returned with some fresh doughnuts.

"Hey!" Ricky laughed. "I said a doughnut . . .
not a doughnut *store*! Please put that
back and bring me some milk!"

Ricky's Robot flew away again.
This time he returned with the
freshest milk he could find.

"Ummm . . ." said Ricky. "I
think I'll skip the milk today!"

CHAPTER SIX
OBEY THE VIDEO VULTURES

After breakfast, the Mighty Robot flew Ricky straight to school. But something was not right!

All the mice in school had strange looks on their faces.

They were all carrying food out the cafeteria door, straight to the center of town.

Ricky found his reading teacher, Miss Swiss.

"What's going on here?" asked Ricky.
"Obey the Video Vultures," said
Miss Swiss.

Then Ricky saw his math teacher, Mr. Mozzarella.

"Aren't we supposed to have a test today?" asked Ricky.

"Obey the Video Vultures," said Mr. Mozzarella.

Finally, Ricky found Principal
Provolone.

"Where is everybody going
with all this food?" asked Ricky.

"Obey the Video Vultures,"
said Principal Provolone.

Ricky was not getting any answers.

"Come on, Robot," said Ricky. "We've got to get to the bottom of this!"

CHAPTER SEVEN
THOSE VICIOUS VULTURES

Ricky and his Mighty Robot followed
the long line of mice to the center of
town. There, they saw a horrible sight!

Victor Von Vulture had taken
over the city and turned everybody
into video slaves. The hungry
Vultures were eating every bite
of food in town.

"We want more chocolate chip cookies!" yelled one of the Vultures.

"Yesss, Video Vultures," said the mice as they scurried off to start baking.

"And no more *rice cakes*!" yelled another Vulture.

"We've got to stop those evil Vultures," Ricky whispered. "But how?"

Ricky and his Mighty Robot looked around. They saw Victor and his evil invention.

"I'll bet those Vultures are controlling everybody with that remote control," said Ricky. "We've got to get it away from them." But that was going to be tricky.

VS-2000

"Hmmm," said Ricky. "What we need is a *distraction*."

CHAPTER EIGHT
RICKY'S RECIPE

Ricky and his Mighty Robot hurried back to school. In the cafeteria kitchen, Ricky mixed together some butter, sugar, and eggs. Then he added flour and chocolate chips.

"Now comes the secret ingredient," said Ricky.

The Mighty Robot flew straight
to Mexico and returned with the
hottest peppers he could find.

Ricky stirred the cookie batter while his Mighty Robot added hundreds of super red-hot chili peppers to the mix.

The Mighty Robot quickly baked
the cookies with his microwave
eyeballs, then cooled the pan with
his super-freezy breath.

CHAPTER NINE
DINNER IS SERVED

Ricky and his Mighty Robot returned
to the center of town. Ricky pretended
he was hypnotized as he bravely
carried his cookies toward the
Video Vultures.

"It's about time!" said one of the Vultures.

"Gimme those cookies!" said another.

The greedy Vultures were fighting over Ricky's cookies. They stuffed them into their mouths as fast as they could.

"OUCHIE! OUCHIE! *OUCHIE!*" screamed the Vultures as they danced around in pain.

Ricky's Mighty Robot grabbed the
Video-Schmideo 2000 and crushed
it in his mighty fist.

Suddenly, all the mice in town returned to normal. They screamed at the sight of the Video Vultures, and everybody ran straight home. Ricky's Mighty Robot had saved the city . . . but Victor Von Vulture had another plan.

CHAPTER TEN
RICKY'S BRIGHT IDEA

Victor Von Vulture knew that Ricky and the Mighty Robot were working together. Quickly, he swooped down and grabbed Ricky. "Don't come any closer, Mighty Robot," said Victor, "or I will destroy your little friend!"

The Video Vultures were very angry. They huffed and they puffed as they surrounded Ricky's Mighty Robot.

"You're going to be sorry you tricked us!" said Victor Von Vulture as he flew higher and higher.

Just when everything seemed
hopeless, Ricky had an idea.

He reached up and grabbed a feather
from Victor Von Vulture's rear end.
Ricky yanked the feather out.

"Ouch!" yelled Victor.

Ricky wiggled the feather
under Victor's claw.

"H-Hey! S-S-Stop that! It tickles!" laughed Victor Von Vulture.

But Ricky did not stop. He wiggled the feather faster and faster. Victor began laughing harder and harder.

Finally, Victor Von Vulture let
go of Ricky. The little mouse fell
through the air. . . .

CHAPTER ELEVEN
ROBO-RESCUE

Ricky was in big trouble. He was falling through the sky, faster and faster. "Help me, Mighty Robot!" Ricky cried.

With lightning speed, the Mighty
Robot's arm shot up into the air. The
Mighty Robot caught Ricky by the
back of his shirt . . .

. . . and set him down safely in a tree.
"Thanks, buddy," said Ricky. "Now
go get 'em!"

CHAPTER TWELVE
THE BATTLE BEGINS

The Mighty Robot flew up and
grabbed Victor in his mighty fist.

"Help, Video Vultures, HELP!!!"
yelled Victor.

Suddenly, the evil Video Vultures got ready to attack. The Mighty Robot was outnumbered.

"This is going to be fun," Victor snarled.

The Video Vultures began to attack.
The Mighty Robot defended himself.

"Hey, wait a minute, Robot," said Victor. "Put me down first!"

But the Mighty Robot did not have time to put Victor down. Victor was stuck in the middle of the fight.

Every time the Mighty Robot
punched, Victor felt the blow!

Every time the Mighty Robot clobbered,
Victor got clobbered, too!

Every time the Mighty Robot clunked heads, Victor got the worst of it!

"Ouchie, ouchie, *ouchie*!" cried Victor Von Vulture. "This is not as much fun as I thought it would be!"

CHAPTER THIRTEEN
THE BIG BATTLE
(IN FLIP-O-RAMA™)

-RAMA

HERE'S HOW IT WORKS!

STEP 1

Place your *left* hand inside the dotted lines marked "LEFT HAND HERE." Hold the book open *flat*.

STEP 2

Grasp the *right-hand* page with your right thumb and index finger (inside the dotted lines marked "RIGHT THUMB HERE").

STEP 3

Now *quickly* flip the right-hand page back and forth until the picture appears to be *animated*.

(For extra fun, try adding your own sound-effects!)

FLIP-O-RAMA 1

(pages 95 and 97)

Remember, flip *only* page 95.
While you are flipping, be sure you
can see the picture on page 95
and the one on page 97.
If you flip quickly, the two
pictures will start to look like
<u>one</u> *animated* picture.

Don't forget to add
your own sound-effects!

LEFT HAND HERE

THE VIDEO
VULTURES ATTACKED.

RIGHT
THUMB
HERE

96

THE VIDEO VULTURES ATTACKED.

FLIP-O-RAMA 2

(pages 99 and 101)

Remember, flip *only* page 99.
While you are flipping, be sure you
can see the picture on page 99
and the one on page 101.
If you flip quickly, the two
pictures will start to look like
<u>one</u> *animated* picture.

Don't forget to add
your own sound-effects!

LEFT HAND HERE

RICKY'S ROBOT
FOUGHT BACK.

RIGHT
THUMB
HERE

**RICKY'S ROBOT
FOUGHT BACK.**

FLIP-O-RAMA 3

(pages 103 and 105)

Remember, flip *only* page 103.
While you are flipping, be sure you
can see the picture on page 103
and the one on page 105.
If you flip quickly, the two
pictures will start to look like
<u>one</u> *animated* picture.

Don't forget to add
your own sound-effects!

LEFT HAND HERE

THE VIDEO VULTURES
BATTLED HARD.

RIGHT
THUMB
HERE

RIGHT
INDEX
FINGER
HERE

THE VIDEO VULTURES
BATTLED HARD.

FLIP-O-RAMA 4

(pages 107 and 109)

Remember, flip *only* page 107.
While you are flipping, be sure you
can see the picture on page 107
and the one on page 109.
If you flip quickly, the two
pictures will start to look like
<u>one</u> animated picture.

Don't forget to add
your own sound-effects!

LEFT HAND HERE

**RICKY'S ROBOT
BATTLED HARDER.**

RIGHT
INDEX
FINGER
HERE

108

RICKY'S ROBOT
BATTLED HARDER.

FLIP-O-RAMA 5

(pages 111 and 113)

Remember, flip *only* page 111.
While you are flipping, be sure you
can see the picture on page 111
and the one on page 113.
If you flip quickly, the two
pictures will start to look like
<u>one</u> *animated* picture.

Don't forget to add
your own sound-effects!

LEFT HAND HERE

AND JUSTICE PREVAILED.

RIGHT
THUMB
HERE

AND JUSTICE PREVAILED.

CHAPTER FOURTEEN
JUSTICE PREVAILS

The evil Video Vultures were no match for Ricky Ricotta's Mighty Robot.

"Let's get out of here!" moaned the Vultures.

"Hey, wait for *ME*!"
cried Victor Von Vulture.
But it was too late.
The Video Vultures flew back to
Venus and were never heard from again.

The Mighty Robot picked up Ricky, and together they took Victor Von Vulture to the Squeakyville jail.

"Boo-hoo-hoo!" cried Victor.

"Maybe now you will learn some responsibility!" said Ricky.

Then Ricky Ricotta and his Mighty
Robot flew straight home . . .

. . . just in time for supper.

CHAPTER FIFTEEN
SUPPERTIME

Ricky's mother and father had cooked a wonderful feast for Ricky and his Mighty Robot.

"Oh, boy!" said Ricky. "TV dinners! My favorite!"

"We're both very proud of you boys," said Ricky's mother.

"Thank you for doing the right thing at the right time," said Ricky's father.

"No problem," said Ricky . . .

. . . "that's what friends are for!"

READY FOR

MORE RICKY?

DAV PILKEY

has written and illustrated more than fifty books for children, including *The Paperboy*, a Caldecott Honor book; *Dog Breath: The Horrible Trouble with Hally Tosis*, winner of the California Young Reader Medal; and the IRA Children's Choice Dumb Bunnies series. He is also the creator of the *New York Times* best-selling Captain Underpants books. Dav lives in the Pacific Northwest with his wife. Find him online at www.pilkey.com.

DAN SANTAT

is the writer and illustrator of the picture book *The Adventures of Beekle: The Unimaginary Friend*. He is also the creator of the graphic novel *Sidekicks* and has illustrated many acclaimed picture books, including the *New York Times* bestseller *Because I'm Your Dad* by Ahmet Zappa and *Crankenstein* by Samantha Berger. Dan also created the Disney animated hit *The Replacements*. He lives in Southern California with his family. Find him online at www.dantat.com.